THE MAGIC ROUNDABOUT ™

STORYBOOK

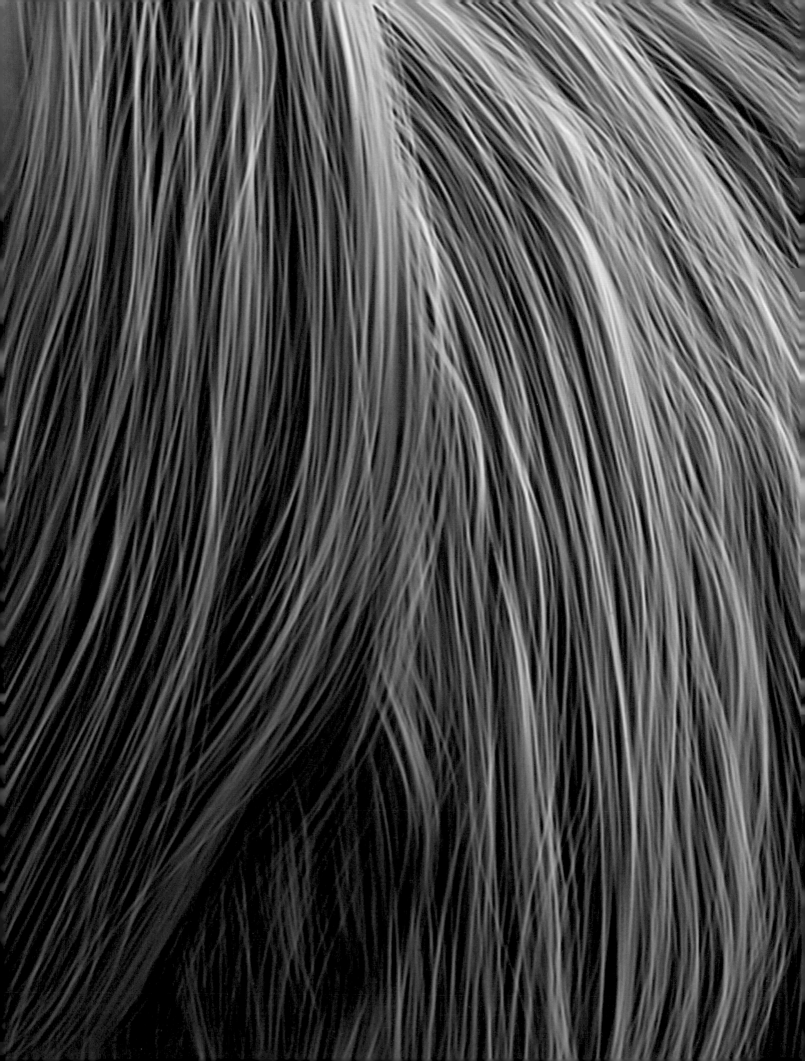

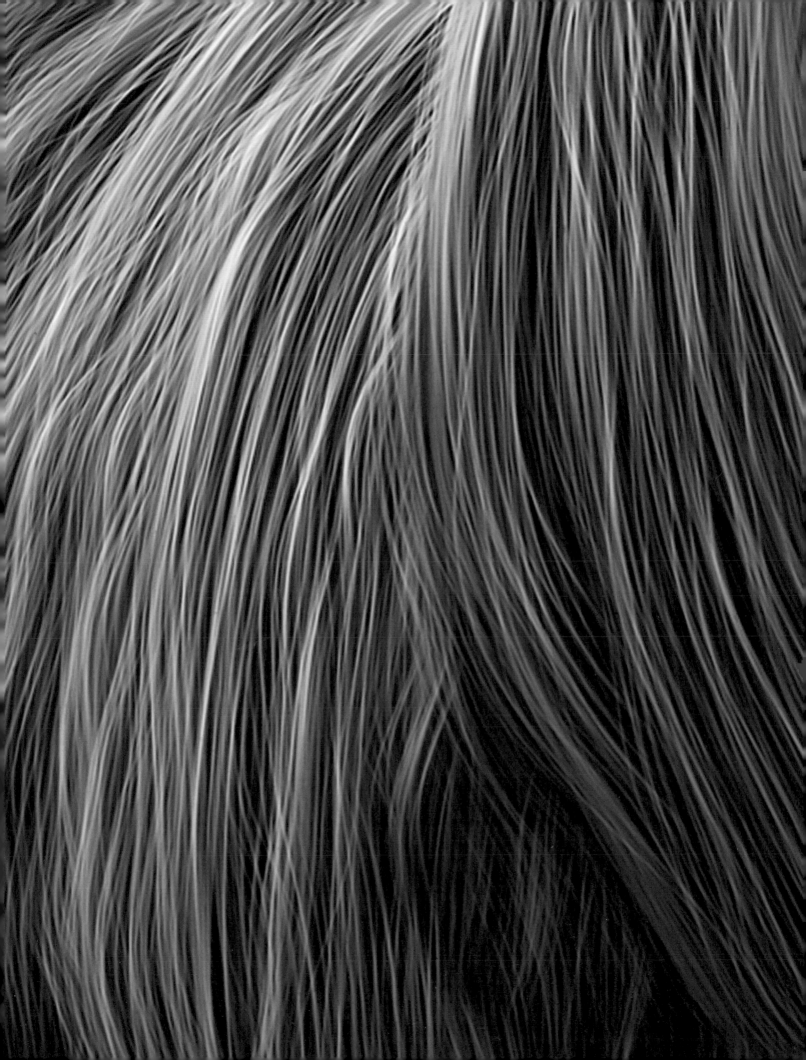

Introducing...

Dougal

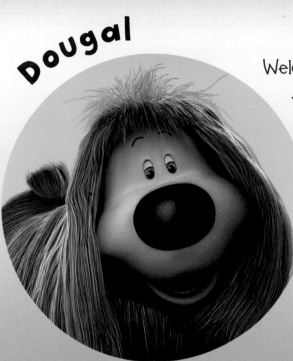

Welcome to our storybook. I don't suppose you brought any sweeties with you? No? A lollipop then? Or a gobstopper perhaps? Oh, well. Good luck – and watch out. Things are gonna get hairy!

Oh, Dougal! You really are a naughty dog. The boys and girls just want to read about your adventure.

Florence

Ermintrude

Yes, well it was that hairy hound who started all the trouble in the first place! Now children, I'm sure you're aware of my fabulous singing talents and you'll be pleased to hear that I am available for weddings, birthday parties or events of any kind. Just talk to my agent.

Brian

Well said,
Ermintrude,
my dear.

Dylan

Hey, Brian! Are you blushing, man?
I think the snail dude likes the
Ermin-dude!

Zebedee

Zipadee-dee, zipedi-da! Oh, here
you all are! Well, let's get started!

Zeebad

And when I'm about
you'd better chill out!

First published in Great Britain in 2005 by HarperCollins Children's Books.
HarperCollins Children's Books is a division of HarperCollins Publishers Ltd.

Creative Consultant Liz Keynes

1 3 5 7 9 10 8 6 4 2

0-00-718355-0

The HarperCollins website address is: www.harpercollinschildrensbooks.co.uk

Printed and bound in Thailand.

"**I**'m going to be late!" panted Dougal as he hurried through the streets of the Enchanted Village.

His fur swished as he sped along. He was on his way somewhere very important...

When Dougal reached the village square, he found everyone had gathered for Ermintrude's special concert.
"Dougal!" smiled Florence, "you're just in time!"
"Er, yes, Florence," replied Dougal in a small voice.

Soon VERY loud singing filled the square but instead of playing along on his guitar, Dylan was dozing off! Ermintrude flicked her tail and woke the sleepy rabbit.

Lalalalalaaaaaaaaaa!

Florence turned to give Dougal a nice pat on the head... but he had disappeared!

Dougal hurried along as fast as he could go. Passing a concert poster, he jumped up to grab a small, sharp drawing pin...

Dougal placed the pin in the middle of the road and hid. The candy-seller would soon pass by on his trike, full of delicious lollipops and chocolates.

"POP!" went the trike's tyre on the sharp pin.

"Oh dear, oh dear!" exclaimed Dougal and he offered to look after the sweeties while the candy-seller went in search of a repair kit.

He was about to help himself to a yummy caramel cream when his furry paw brushed against the trike's gear stick. Whoops! The trike took off at high speed, heading straight for the Village!

"Whooooooa! Heeelp!" cried Dougal, falling off with a bump. Crash, the trike smashed into The Magic Roundabout as everyone watched helplessly. The roof of The Roundabout exploded!

"Puccini preserve us!" cried Ermintrude.

With Florence and the children still clinging on, The Roundabout began to turn faster and faster. A strange icy mist swirled all around.

"It's out of control!" shouted Mr Rusty.

Another shudder, and two shadowy shapes catapaulted out of the hole in The Roundabout's roof, to land on a far away mountainside! Before long, The Roundabout was frozen solid, with Florence and the children trapped inside!

"Zebedee! Zebedee! Zebedee!" cried Dougal, Dylan, Brian and Ermintrude in unison.

BOING!

When Zebedee arrived he was horrified... "I hoped this day would never come. The day Zeebad escapes! He is an evil springer with incredible magic powers, and only by returning three enchanted diamonds to The Roundabout will you defeat him. But if he finds them first, he will use them to freeze the sun for ever.

Nothing will grow, not even grass! One of the diamonds is here and I must stay behind to guard it. To find the other two, you will need this map."

Meanwhile, far away on a snowy mountainside... the two shadowy figures landed.

"Free at last!" Zeebad smiled wickedly. "Soon it will be nice and frozen everywhere!"

A crackle of icy magic zapped from his moustache. A moose grazing nearby turned bright blue and galloped off!

Another spark zapped towards a toy soldier half-buried in the snow. At once the toy soldier grew bigger and saluted his new master.

"Soldier Sam, SIR! Reporting for duty."

Back in the Enchanted Village, Zebedee took out a magic box and pressed a big green button. Instantly, a little red Train appeared with a jolly **'toot toot.'**

"Take good care of this little box," said Zebedee, handing the magic box to Dylan.

"Don't worry, Florence, we're going to get you out of there!" promised Dougal as they climbed aboard the Train and set off to find the diamonds.

On the way Dougal tried to explain to his friends about the crashed trike and the wrecked Roundabout.

"I only wanted to get my teeth into some sweeties," he pleaded.

But they were all very cross with him and that night his friends left him alone to keep watch over the camp.

"Why do I have to be the guard dog?" he whined. "What's wrong with a guard cow?"

In the morning, Dougal was nowhere to be seen.

"Dooooooooougal?" they shouted hopelessly.

Zeebad had captured Dougal in the night and imprisoned him in his ice palace. "Now, you dim-witted draught excluder, tell

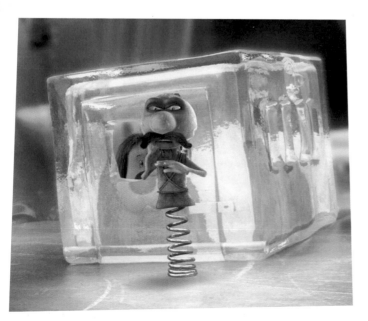

me everything!" he demanded.

"Me? I don't know anything. I don't even have the map!" cried Dougal.

"So there's a map, eh? Sam, torture this boarding house for fleas until he tells us everything!" ordered Zeebad.

Soldier Sam had never tortured anyone before so he asked Dougal what he was afraid of. Dougal knew just what to say. SUGAR! And he was now munching happily on his twenty-seventh sugar lump.

"NO! Please, don't...no more, please..." he moaned, pretending to be in terrible pain.

Zeebad listened to the moans and groans with glee.

"Mwah, ha ha ha! Soon the diamonds will be mine!" he sniggered horribly.

Meanwhile, a little help from the friendly blue moose had led Dougal's friends to Zeebad's cave. The gang made a clever plan to rescue Dougal. Carefully, Ermintrude was lowered through the roof. THUD! She landed right on top of Soldier Sam!

"After them!"

called Zeebad as he spotted the rescuers escaping through the roof. Slipping and sliding along a snowy pathway as fast as they could, the chase led them to the edge of a very tall cliff!

"Whoooooa, that is deep!" said Dylan.

"Zebedee!
Zebedee!
Zebedee!"

they called desperately!

"Zipadi-dee, zipadi-da!"
sang Zebedee, springing
to the scene.

"YOU!" growled
Zeebad menacingly.

Zeebad fired an icy blast, just missing
Zebedee's spring. The old enemies flew
into a mighty battle.
"Run, everybody!" warned Zebedee, just
as one of Zeebad's icy rays froze him to
the cliff's edge.

"Zebedee's in trouble!" cried Dougal.

Too late, they watched in horror as
Zeebad blasted away the cliff edge
beneath Zebedee and their friend
fell far, far below.

"Get the diaaaaaaaaaamooonds!"
he cried.

The friends turned and ran for their lives.

The group chugged sadly across a snowy landscape.

"Now who's going to help Florence and the children?" worried Dougal.

"Who's going to help us?" wailed Ermintrude.

"We have to be brave and find the diamonds," Brian reminded them.

"That's the spirit, Brian!" piped up Dougal, trying to sound brave. "Nothing short of a sea of boiling lava will keep me from that diamond! Now where's the map?"

"Oh, sugar," said Dougal gloomily, looking at a sea of boiling lava. The map had led them to the top of a volcano! "Well, that's where the first diamond is," said Ermintrude, pointing to a stone tower in the middle.

A tiny bridge crossed over the lava field to the tower.

Trembling, Train edged forward, but the bridge started to crumble like a broken biscuit! Train's wagon slid off with Dougal and Ermintrude still in it! "Whoa...Dylan...heeelp!" they shrieked. Seconds...ticked...by. "I'm totally not train trained," said Dylan as he finally found the right button and Train pulled itself back onto the bridge. Ahead of them, there it was! Dylan reached out and took the first enchanted diamond!

Then, to their amazement, inside the sparkling blue stone, a vision of The Magic Roundabout appeared! Sniffing back tears, they watched poor Florence and the children shivering inside. They were freezing fast!

Moments later, Zeebad POUNCED and SWIPED the diamond.

"And I'll take the map too," he growled.

"How does he know about the map?" asked Brian.

Dougal looked at the ground.

"They tortured it out of me!" he declared.

"You only get the map over my dead body," said Brian bravely.

"Request granted! Get out the garlic butter," ordered Zeebad.

"Leave him alone. Take the map," said Ermintrude angrily.

So they did, and left, smashing the bridge to bits behind them.

With no bridge, it seemed there was no way out for the gang, until Dylan remembered the magic box. He pressed the button and 'poof', Train's wagon turned into a boat! They sighed with disappointment. What use was a boat on top of a volcano?

"Wait! I've got it!" said Dylan. Working quickly, he pulled their tents together to transform the boat into a hot air balloon!

"My, you are clever!" said Ermintrude as they took to the sky.
"We still have no idea where we're going," sniffed Brian.
"Brian's right. We could drift around for years!" Dougal added.
"Or we could just, like, follow them?" suggested Dylan sleepily.

Far below, in an old
rowing boat, Zeebad
was making for the
second diamond.
"Row faster, you wooden
windbag!" he cursed.
"Yes sir," answered Sam.

Zeebad and Sam arrived at
a temple in the jungle.
"This is definitely the place,"
said Zeebad, checking the map
carefully. Suddenly, a very
sharp stick sprang out of
nowhere, just missing Sam's
head. Booby traps!

Zeebad looked up to see the
balloon boat coming down just
outside the temple entrance.
"They're still alive?" he
complained. "No matter.
Booby traps need a bunch
of boobies. We'll let them clear
the way!"

The balloon boat landed with a bump and everyone tumbled
out. Dougal led the way into the temple as a spear WHOOSHED
past his nose! Now leading the way did not seem
a very good idea. No-one wanted to go first.
"Oh, for heaven's sake. I'll go!" Brian said.
And with that he slid forward narrowly
avoiding rocks, spears, snakes and
arrows, muttering grumpily to himself
all the way.

Inside the old temple was a great throne room.

"The perfect place to enjoy my last gobstopper," said Dougal cheerfully as he climbed the magnificent stone throne.

"Oh, great, a recline button!" He pressed a button on the arm rest. With a low rumble, a stone altar shot up through the temple floor. A claw held a sparkling yellow diamond! Instantly, light beams criss-crossed the room.

"They're alarm beams! " shouted Brian.

In moments, clever Ermintrude took to the floor and she bent, twisted and leapt like a ballet dancer over and under the alarm beams, all the way to the diamond!

"Well done! That was brill..." said Dougal brightly as the gobstopper flew out of his mouth! "Whoops!" he added as it broke through an alarm beam!

With a crash, four ninja skeletons burst through the floor!
"I don't suppose anyone knows anything about martial arts?" gasped Ermintrude.
"Just the basics of kung-fu, karate, judo, kendo, tai-kwan-do, anything-you-can-do... and tai-chi," replied Dylan lazily.
"Ooooooh...do those come with egg fried rice?" drooled Dougal.
"Dylan! Can you beat them up?" asked Brian, just as a skeleton flung a flying kick at Dylan's head.
"Only in self defence," Dylan replied, smashing the skeleton against a wall with a cool kung-fu chop.

When Dylan had finished, all that remained of the four skeletons were heaps of bones.

"Good group effort," said Dougal. "Let's get the diamond." But behind him, the skeleton bones twitched and slid together, this time into

ONE GIANT MONSTER SKELETON!

"Heeeeelp! Dogs are meant to eat bones, not the other way around!" cried Dougal as he raced around the room, followed by the monster.

Just in time, Dougal hopped onto the throne and desperately pressed a button with his nose. Suddenly the floor beneath the skeleton disappeared sending it crashing through the hole into the darkness below.

"Let's grab the diamond and get out of here!" gulped Dougal. But the diamond had GONE!

"Zeebad must have followed us...but only we know where the final diamond is," said Dougal, just as an evil cackle sounded behind him. Zeebad was holding the second diamond!

"Now tell me where the third diamond is!" he shouted.

"Dougal! Now!" squealed Ermintrude.

Dougal dashed to the throne and pressed the button again. Zeebad and Sam tumbled down into the hole.

"Hooray!" the gang cheered.

"Back to The Roundabout as fast as we can!" called Ermintrude.

Dylan heard a friendly **'toot-toot'**. Train to the rescue!
And coming up fast behind it, another train with Zeebad
and Sam aboard!

"Where's my last diamond?" screamed Zeebad as Sam stoked the red hot boiler.

Dylan looked at the train's controls.
"An anti-spring device. This'll
slow Zeebad down..."
he said hopefully.
But it was an ejector seat!
Unlucky Brian was pinged
upwards, landing with a bump
on the roof of Zeebad's train.

"Did we reach The Roundabout yet?" called out the dazed snail.

"So that's where you're headed!" shouted Zeebad triumphantly.

Using her tail as a rope, Ermintrude made a dramatic rescue, and swung Brian back aboard Train.

But by now, Zeebad's train was glowing red hot. With a great bang, the engine exploded and the two passengers were flung into the distant hills.

But it was the end of the line for the little red Train too. It crashed into the buffers and dog, cow, rabbit and snail were thrown high into the sky.

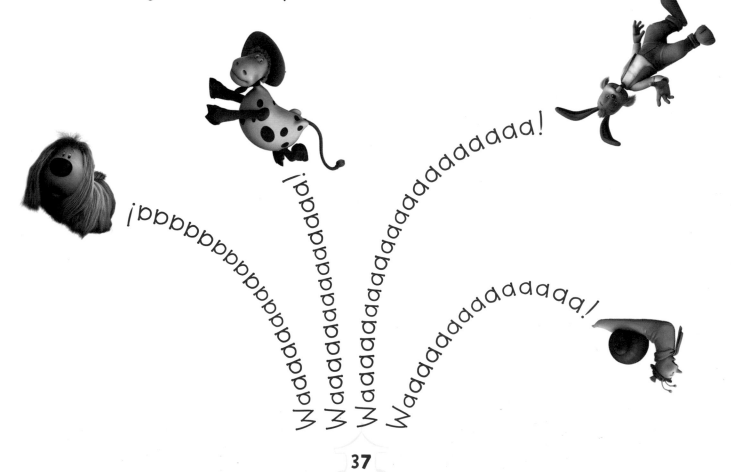

THUD! THUD! THUD, THUD! THUD!

The five landed heavily on a snowy hilltop. "We must get back to The Roundabout before Zeebad", said Brian.

"Hang on, Zeebad doesn't know the diamond is at The Roundabout," said Dougal.

Brian blushed and admitted, "Back there...on the train...it just slipped out!"

Poor damaged Train gave a weak 'toot' but could not keep up.

"Oh, poor Trainy!" sighed Ermintrude sadly.

"You can make it. Just follow our tracks!" said Brian, as they set off on foot.

On they went until they were so tired that they curled up in the snow and fell fast asleep.

The next morning, the sun shone down and woke up the sleepy friends – and they saw the Enchanted Village just a short walk away!

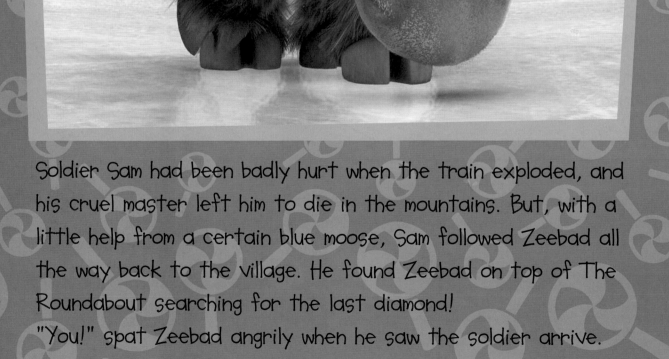

Soldier Sam had been badly hurt when the train exploded, and his cruel master left him to die in the mountains. But, with a little help from a certain blue moose, Sam followed Zeebad all the way back to the village. He found Zeebad on top of The Roundabout searching for the last diamond!

"You!" spat Zeebad angrily when he saw the soldier arrive.

"It's time for me to resume my post, guarding The Magic Roundabout from the likes of you!" said Sam grimly.

"You were on The Roundabout?" sneered Zeebad, firing a huge blast at the soldier. WHAM! Sam's chest split open and a bright light shone out.

"The diamond! And to think I left you to die!" laughed Zeebad, and he grabbed the stone.

"So long, sunshine!"

Now Zeebad joined the power of the three diamonds together and slowly ice began to creep over the face of the sun!

The gang arrived.

"Too late! We're doomed!" gasped Brian.

"This is all my fault!" wailed Dougal.

Dylan was furious. "You're seriously messing with my karma. Eat this!" he shouted at Zeebad, hurling a snowball. Zeebad turned and aimed his moustache to zap Dylan.

"Aaaaaaaaaaaaaaaaaaaaaaaah!"

screamed out Ermintrude's powerful voice as a stinging beam struck her on the tail. Dougal blinked. He was sure he could see a tiny crack in the frozen Roundabout! He had an idea.

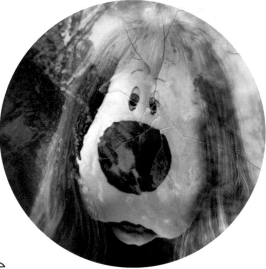

"That's it! Ermintrude, sing! Sing!"

Ermintrude sang even louder, and sure enough, bigger cracks snaked across the ice. Dougal, Dylan and Brian dived for the diamonds, ducking and dodging Zeebad's deadly blasts. With an amazing display of teamwork, two diamonds were slotted into their proper spaces on The Roundabout. But Zeebad still had the third diamond! To everyone's surprise 'toot-toot!' Train rushed into the village flattening Zeebad under its wheels and sending the last diamond sailing high into the air.

Like a top class footballer, Dougal headed it into place.

"Noooooooooooooooooooooooooo!" raged Zeebad, as he was sucked deep down into a vortex at the centre of the earth along with all the ice and snow he had brought with him.

"We did it!" the friends cheered happily.
"Of course we did it, darlings. There's nothing like opera for breaking the ice!" trilled Ermintrude.

Shivering, the children stepped off The Magic Roundabout. But Florence did not move. Dougal ran to her side and frantically licked her frozen face. Her eyelids fluttered. Hooray, she was alive!

Far away, at the foot of a mountain, Zebedee too sprung to life and bounced back to The Roundabout to join the others.

"Bravo my friends. Everyone knows that after winter it's time for SPRING!"

But someone was NOT happy!

"Curses! Imprisoned once more!

muttered Zeebad.

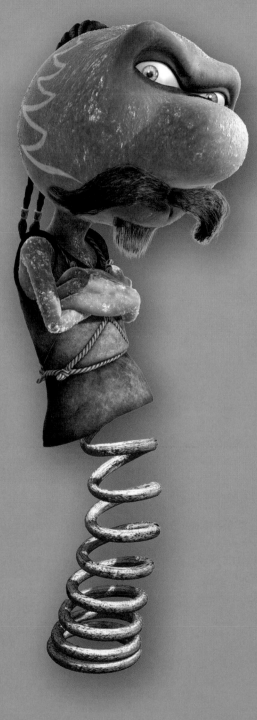

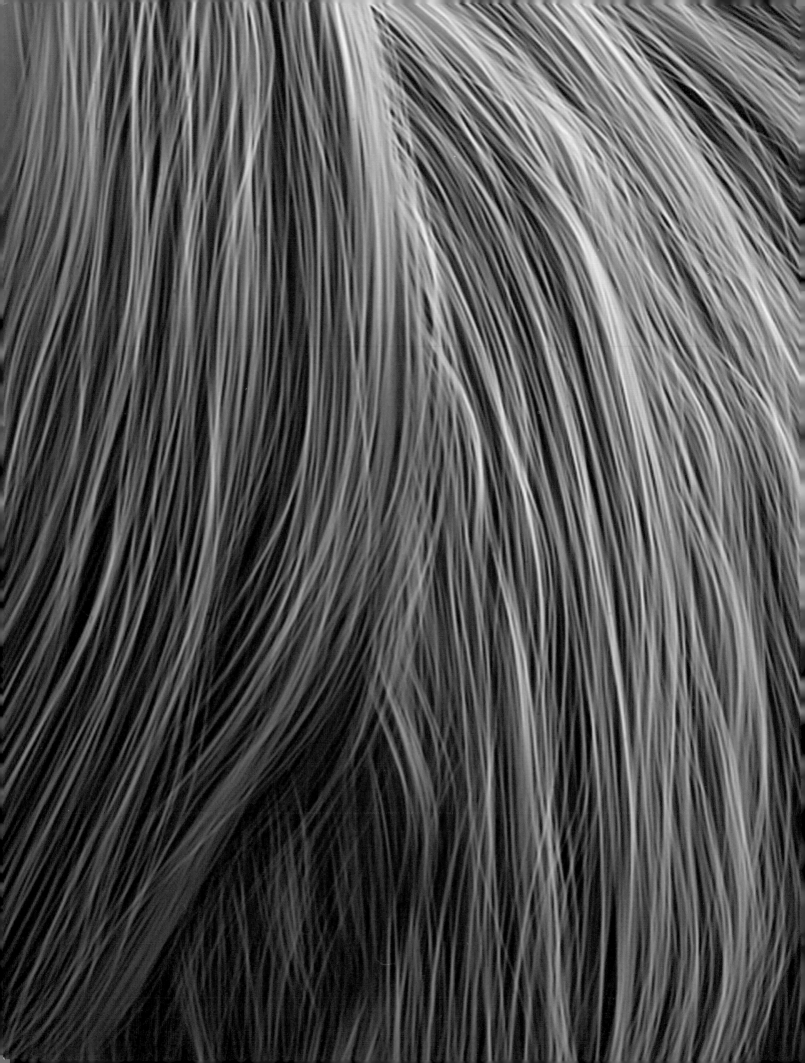

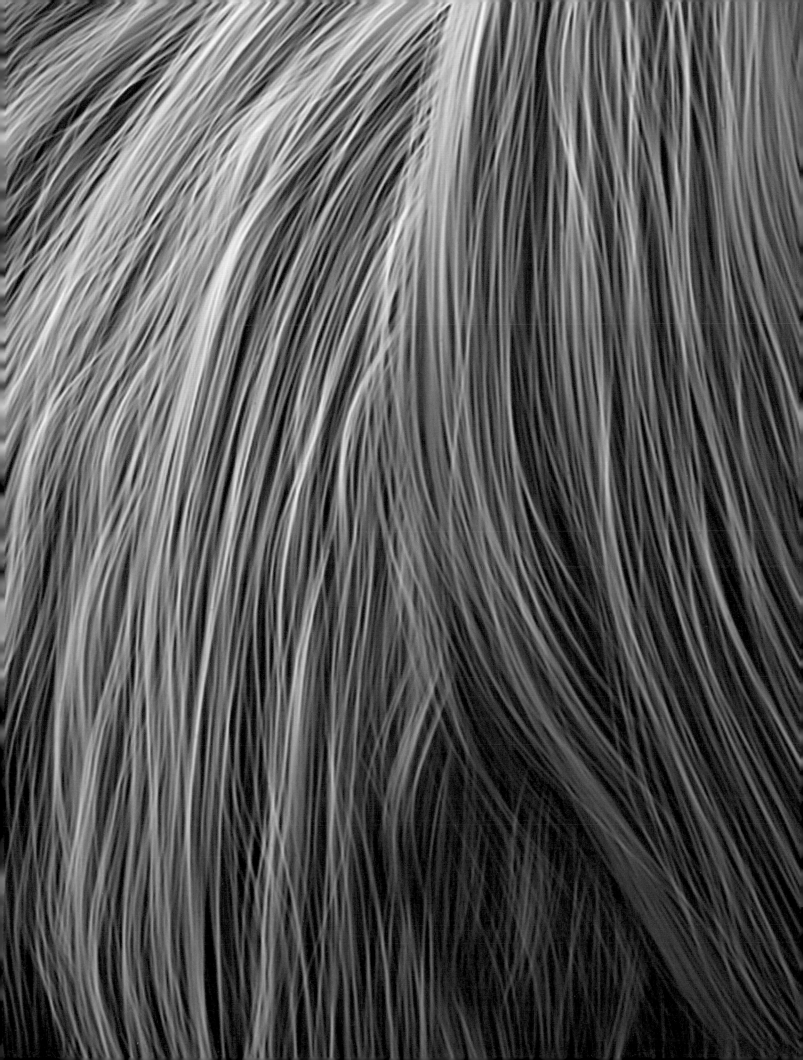

THE MAGIC ROUNDABOUT

There's more to this rabbit than meets the eye!

Light Activated Room Guard DYLAN™

Gift Boxed Mugs

Coming soon to all good toy & gift shops

Bouncing ZEBEDEE™

Zebedee still has some spring in his step!

Character Beanies

Lots of fun sounds and silly phrases!

Talk'n Sing ERMINTRUDE™

Press my tummy to hear me talk!

Talking FLORENCE™

ERMINTRUDE™ **Back Pack**

See Dougal™ spin on the spot!

Remote Control DOUGAL™

Colour and specification may change.